Now You See Me...

NOW YOU SEE ME . . .
A BANTAM BOOK 978 0 857 51043 3

Published in Great Britain by Bantam,
an imprint of Random House Children's Books
A Random House Group Company

This edition published 2011

1 3 5 7 9 10 8 6 4 2

Bantam Books are published by Random House Children's Books,
61–63 Uxbridge Road, London W5 5SA

www.**seussville**.com
www.**kids**at**randomhouse**.co.uk

Addresses for companies within The Random House Group Limited can be found at:
www.randomhouse.co.uk/offices.htm

THE RANDOM HOUSE GROUP Limited Reg. No. 954009

A CIP catalogue record for this book is available from the British Library

Printed in Italy

Now You See Me...

By Tish Rabe
based on a television script
by Katherine Standford
Illustrated by Christopher Moroney

BANTAM BOOKS

Nick said, "It's the holidays!
And we have all week
to play games and have fun.
Want to play hide-and-seek?"

"You count and I'll hide,"
Sally said. "And you'll see –
I'll hide so well that
you'll never find me!"

Sally looked till she found
a good hiding spot.
". . . Ten!" Nick called out.
"Coming! Ready or not!"

Where was Sally hiding?
In less than a minute,
Nick ran to the wheelbarrow
and found Sally in it!

"Hide-and-seek!" cried the Cat.
"Oh, I'm so glad I came!
The counting! The hiding!
It's my favourite game!"
"It's great!" Nick agreed.
Sally said as she sighed,
"But Nick always finds me
wherever I hide."

"Aha!" said the Cat.
"We must leave right away
to meet my friend Gecko,
who plays every day.

He hides in the day
and also at night.
It helps him stay safe
to keep out of sight."

So they flew to the jungle.

It was steamy and hot.

"My friend," said the Cat,

"is not easy to spot.

Cam-ou-flage helps him hide.

It is his hiding trick."

"Cam-ou-*what*? I don't know

what that word means!" said Nick.

"I'll explain," said the Cat. "Camouflage is the way some animals stay out of sight every day.

Camouflage helps them hide

so they will not be found.

It helps them blend in

with whatever's around."

"That Gecko blends in.
He's not easy to see."
"Hello!" Gecko called.
"Are you looking for me?
My tail looks leaf-like
and my skin is light brown.
I'm hanging right here in
this tree upside down!"

"Could you show us," asked Sally,
"how to hide like you do?
We want to learn how
to use camouflage too!"
"In the jungle," said Gecko,
"your clothes are too bright.
You need to blend in
so you stay out of sight."

"We can't hide dressed like this,"
said Nick. "What to do?"
"You need help," said the Cat,
"from Thing One and Thing Two!"
"Can you help us," asked Sally,
"look leafy and green?
If we look like the jungle,
we'll never be seen."

So, before the kids knew it,

they got a surprise –

Things One and Two made

them the perfect disguise!

"Mr. Gecko," said Nick,
"you can hide, it is true.
But can you find us
when we're hiding from *you*?"

"Of course!" Gecko said, but when he looked around, those camouflaged kids were nowhere to be found!

He looked in the shadows
and looked in the light.
They were hiding so well
they were nowhere in sight.

Then all of a sudden
a tree started to wiggle.
"Wait!" Gecko said.
"I just heard someone giggle!
Out here in the jungle,"
he said with a smile,
"the trees haven't giggled
in quite a long while."

"Nick," Sally asked,
"when I was hiding today,
how did you find where
I was right away?"
"Well," Nick said, "finding
you wasn't hard.
Your dress was the only pink
thing in my yard."

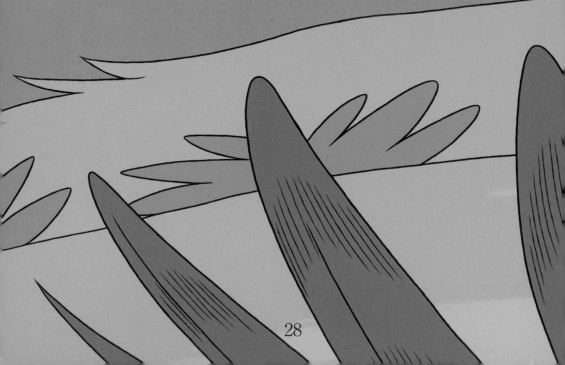

"Hide-and-seek," said the Cat,
"is so much fun to play.
I could play it with Gecko
and you every day.

But we have to go now.

We'll be back soon, I know.

Goodbye, Gecko!

Oh . . . Gecko?"

"NOW where did he go?"